THE VAMPIRE'S VICTIM

SHAWN WISEMAN

No part of this book may be reproduced, scanned, or distributed in any printed or electronic form without written permission from the author of this novel.

This is a work of fiction. Any similarity to persons, living or dead, is purely coincidental.

TABLE OF CONTENTS

1. THE RELUCTANT HELPER

Kara held the pipe in her hand as she leaned out the window of her room. She sucked in the smoke, filling her lungs, and then exhaled. The marijuana's burning essence and chemicals rushed through her body, making her feel elated. It also helped her let go of unpleasant thoughts, if but for a moment. The only part she didn't like was that she could feel her psychic powers dull. She knew that if she wanted to use her powers, she would have to focus that much harder to do so.

Kara took another puff and exhaled it out her window, making sure to not let any smoke touch her room or clothes.

"Kara! When are we eating?" The gravelly voice of Magnus Montgomery filtered through her closed door.

"It's in the slow cooker," Kara yelled over her shoulder. "I'll be right out, but feel free to dish it out yourself."

Kara thought she could hear some mumbling, and maybe even some grumbling, from beyond the wooden doorframe. She smirked as she thought of the exact look on Magnus's face just then. She extinguished the burning embers and put away the pipe she had been using.

After giving herself a once-over for smell, she went into the living room and kitchen. She scooped out some chili from the slow cooker and sat down across from Magnus at the table.

The old man's wrinkled features were obscured by the black and grey pages of a newspaper, which he occasionally flipped after clinking a spoon against an equally obscured bowl. Kara, the younger of the two despite her being the near-immortal vampire, pulled out her more advanced news device, her smartphone, and played on it while she ate.

Kara couldn't help but reflect on how she enjoyed times like this. Though their communication was infrequent, and he didn't know about her supernatural side, she felt that they shared a bond. They didn't need to talk, as they could just enjoy each other's silent company.

Maybe it's just the weed making me feel this way. I'll have to thank James for that if I ever see him again… after I give him another punch in the face, of course.

As Kara was staring at Magnus, she felt something creeping up at her from the back of her head. The feeling of dread flooded over her in a wave until it reached her fingertips and toes. The foreboding feeling washed away her happiness in an instant with its familiar grasp.

As clear as day, when Kara closed her eyes, she could see the image of Magnus lying on the carpeted floor of the apartment, dead. No blood, no visible injuries, just dead for an unknown reason. When she opened them, Magnus was in front of her still reading the newspaper. The contrast was jarring, to say the least, and she couldn't shake the feeling gripping her heart.

"Mr. Montgomery, are you feeling well today?" she asked.

"Of course I am. Never better," he replied without moving the paper.

Despite his assurances, the image of his death didn't leave her mind. The feeling she had wasn't as strong as when she felt Olivia's immediate death a week before. She couldn't tell when exactly her premonition would come true, or even if it would. Mr. Montgomery had an uncanny ability to defy her foresight time and time again.

"I think we should make an appointment for you to get a checkup," she suggested.

Magnus moved the paper out of the way, revealing his frowning face. "I told you I'm fine. Besides," he said while he pulled out a flask, "I have my medicine right here." He smirked as he opened the flask and took a swig. He chuckled as he re-opened his newspaper.

Kara couldn't help but also smile at Mr. Montgomery's good spirits, and soon the feeling of dread that came over her went away.

She continued to eat and play on her phone until she received a text message from Raymond. He asked to come over for something, and Kara replied that he could come over anytime. A minute after she sent her reply, there was a knock at the door.

Kara looked at the door and raised her brows. *It can't be,* she thought.

She got up and opened the door, and sure enough, Raymond was there waiting. Her vampire friend somehow looked more gloomy than

The Vampire's Victim

usual. His normal ghostly pallor was tinted with black bags under his eyes. He adjusted his glasses and glanced from Kara to Mr. Montgomery, who had one eye on him over his shoulder.

"Ray, I didn't expect you for a while. Were you just waiting outside?"

Raymond smiled sheepishly for a moment and ran his fingers through his hair. "I came over and then thought I should ask you if it was alright. Sorry."

Kara waved her hand. "No, no, it's alright. Come in," she said, moving out of the way.

Raymond eyed Mr. Montgomery for a moment, and then he walked inside.

Kara took Raymond's coat and put it inside a closet near the door. "Did you want some chili? It's been simmering all day in the slow cooker. It's pretty good, if I do say so myself," she said with a proud grin.

Raymond looked at the slow cooker with longing, and Kara could tell he wanted some of her cooking. "I shouldn't."

His answer shocked her, and she would be lying if she said she wasn't disappointed. She brushed it off, and motioned for Raymond to join her on the couch.

The two of them sat down to talk. "So, Raymond, what was so urgent?"

Raymond continued to glance at Magnus, but soon, with clear trepidation, answered her question. "...Damien left, and I'm not sure where he went. None of the others know where he is either."

Kara was taken aback, and had many questions, not the least of which was, "Why are you coming to me for help? I'm sure there are other people more qualified to help find Damien than me."

"Well... " he started, scratching his face, "you two were close. I figure if anyone would know what he was thinking, or have some idea on how to find him, it would be you."

Kara sighed. *He's not wrong.* Damien being her ex meant that she would know him intimately, and she might know a way to find him, but her curiosity needed to be satisfied first. "So, can you give me a rundown of what happened before he left? And did he say he was going, or is he actually missing?"

3

Raymond shuffled on the couch. "Well, he did say that he was going, but he didn't say why. I think it had something to do with the incident that happened a week ago," Raymond said, looking over his shoulder at Magnus, who was still reading the newspaper.

"What about the incident makes you think that?" Kara asked with her brow raised.

"Well, he pressed me for more information on what happened after I got back to our house, and I had to tell him everything, including the person who hired... you know who."

Kara grumbled. *If I know Damien, he's probably going after that detective now.* "So, you think he's after that person?"

"Yeah, when I mentioned the name, his expression changed. The day after he said he was going out. That was three days ago now."

"It seems like something he would do," Kara commented. "So you haven't had any contact with him since?"

"I've been messaging him, but he's not responding. I know he has his phone on him, though, because he read one of my messages I sent on social media."

Kara nodded. "Read notifications are rather handy in situations like this, I suppose."

"I don't think he wants to involve anyone, and just wants to do this on his own. That's why he's not responding to me."

"It's obvious he wants revenge, though I'm not sure why he waited until now," Kara said as she rubbed her chin. "Well, I think I have a way to find him. Come with me." She got up off the couch.

She took Raymond to her room. They entered the dirty space, and Kara went to her computer. Raymond had to tip-toe past the various dirty clothes on the floor, and took a seat on the edge of the unmade bed. The smoke from her previous activities lingered in the small room and Raymond couldn't help but cough and attempt to disperse the vapour with a wave of his hand.

Kara brought up a find-a-phone page, then entered Damien's phone number. *I wonder if he's changed the password. Not likely.* Kara tried a password she knew he used to use, and then pressed enter. The next page started to load, and she couldn't help but grin to herself. *What a dummy,* she thought, but at the same time her cheeks reddened.

"You know his password?" Raymond asked.

4

The Vampire's Victim

His voice startled her back to reality, and she let out an involuntary laugh. "Yeah, I thought he might still be using the same one. He was never one to change his passwords."

Raymond scoffed. "Cyber-security isn't his priority. What was his password, if you don't mind my asking? It could be useful if I had it as well."

Kara's face flushed again despite her stark white vampire complexion. "I don't know if I should say..." she replied while scratching her face.

Raymond looked at her and grinned. "With a face like that, now you *have* to tell me."

Kara sighed, and then mumbled something under her breath. When Raymond pressed her she said the password aloud. "Kara420blazeit."

Raymond had to take a moment to register what he heard, and when he did he burst out in an uncontrollable fit of laughter. He put his hand on his stomach as he snickered.

At first Kara was embarrassed, but after a moment she joined in laughing with Raymond.

Between his dying laughter, Raymond asked, "Why would he have that as a password?"

"It was to make fun of me, but of course it wasn't meant as an insult."

Raymond was still smiling. "No, no, of course not. It's very... cute."

Kara shook her head and pushed Raymond as she continued laughing from embarrassment. After another moment, and a sigh from both of them, Kara went back to the computer.

The page had loaded, and it showed the GPS location of Damien's phone. It was in an urban housing district in downtown.

"Well, there you go. Now you know where he is," she said, turning around in her chair again. "Need anything else?"

Raymond raised his brow. "Aren't... Aren't you going to come with me to find him?"

Kara lost her smile. "I don't think he'd want to see me."

"I think I already established that he doesn't want to see anyone right now," Raymond countered with a slight smile. "I could use your help still. I don't know what he's doing, and if it's something dangerous it'd be nice if you had my back."

Kara frowned and looked away from Raymond.

"I'm sorry, you know," he said.

Kara looked at him, and his chin was hitting his chest as he gazed at the floor. "For what?"

"I killed that man in front of you. I know you've been holed up here ever since then. I just didn't see any other way it could have gone. I'm sorry that I killed him when you were trying to talk him down."

Kara placed her hand on Raymond's knee and gave it a squeeze. "Raymond, if anything, I should be thanking you. He wasn't listening, and if you didn't kill him either I would have had to or he would have killed us." Kara let go of Raymond's leg, and looked off in thought. "Besides, it was just that house. I think it was leftover psychic energy that overwhelmed me. I guess I'm sensitive to that stuff now."

"So you're not mad at me?"

"No, of course not," she replied. "I just… I don't know if I can take Damien's shit right now."

Raymond pointed his thumb at himself. "Don't worry. I'll make sure he doesn't say anything."

Kara couldn't help but smile at Raymond's confidence. "Alright, I'll help you out," she said. Raymond smiled and thanked her. Kara rose from her computer chair. "Let's go find Damien!"

2. FANGS IN THE NIGHT

"So, Olivia's having her surgery?" Raymond asked.

"Yeah, she's getting it done today, and she's taking the day off tomorrow. We're on our own tonight."

Raymond frowned. "Well, let's hope nothing bad happens."

"I'm sure it'll be fine," Kara reassured him. "I'm also interested in Detective Simmons. Maybe we'll be able to learn why he's after us."

"That's if Damien hasn't killed him already."

"Let's hope not."

Kara and Raymond entered his vehicle and drove to the urban neighbourhood the GPS pointed them to. Kara kept the GPS open on her phone just in case Damien moved. Traffic slowed them down considerably, and by the time they arrived it was getting dark. The days were colder as winter approached, and night came sooner than normal.

As the GPS wasn't one hundred percent accurate, Raymond had to circle around some of the blocks to find their mark. They passed by tall and thin brick and wooden houses placed side by side on the street. People were walking underneath trees with spindly branches covered in coloured leaves, and cars lined the street, allowing no room for newcomers to park.

"There!" Kara shouted while pointing off to one side of the street. "There's his car."

As they passed by, the two of them stared into the windows of Damien's car and they could see him in the front seat. He was trying to remain hidden behind the metal parts around the doors. His eyes widened as they drove past; he'd noticed them.

"Find us a parking spot and we'll walk back."

"Already on it," Raymond replied.

They managed to find a parking spot a block away, and then they walked back to where Damien was parked.

Kara tried to enter the car, but the door was locked. She bent over and knocked on the window. Damien waved his hand at her, trying to shoo her away. She frowned and furrowed her brows in her best "are you serious?" face, and then she pointed to the lock.

He gave her an angry look, and then rolled down the window. "Go away!" he spat before rolling up the window again.

"Screw this," Kara said aloud.

She used her telekinesis to open the lock on the door and got inside. Damien did a double take as she sat down and closed the door. She clicked the button to unlock the other doors, and Raymond entered the back seat.

"What the fuck are you guys doing here? You're going to get me caught!"

Damien went back to looking out the window towards the other side of the street.

"I should ask you the same question. What are you doing chasing after Detective Simmons? You want to get yourself killed?"

Damien turned around and looked astonished. "How did you know I was going after Simmons?"

Kara rolled her eyes. "Oh come on, you think it was that hard to figure out? Ray tells you about how Simmons sent someone after us again, and you disappear. It's not much of a stretch."

Damien looked furious, and he directed some of that anger at Raymond. "Why'd you go and tell her, Raymond?"

"Maybe if you texted me back I wouldn't have worried about you so much," he retorted.

Damien clenched his teeth and turned his attention back to the house he was watching. "So what about it? I'd rather try and attack him and get killed than wait around for him to send another of his goons after us... and I didn't want to involve you guys."

Kara's voice softened. "We're already involved. We have a right to be party to this. I know you're just trying to be chivalrous, but you're endangering yourself when we could be working together."

There was a brief pause before Damien responded. "Yeah, well, I don't care. You should leave before you blow my cover."

The Vampire's Victim

Kara and Raymond looked at each other. Raymond couldn't help but laugh, and Kara sputtered a few snickers as well. "You're not doing the best job as it is. People on the street can see you."

Damien growled. "It's not like I can help how big I am or where I can park. This is the only place I found where I could see the detective's home."

"Why are you watching him anyway?" Kara asked. "If you were going to attack I thought you would have done it already."

"I only just found his home address. I thought the guy would go out last night, and I was going to attack him then, but he didn't. I changed plans and was going to bust into his home after he goes to sleep."

"And what are you planning to do? Scare him? Kill him?" Kara asked.

Damien glanced over his shoulder at Kara, his face stone. "I don't know."

Kara could tell he was holding back. Raymond had said he told Damien about what happened with the assassin, so he no doubt also mentioned her meltdown when Raymond killed him.

"You should leave," Damien said while looking across the street.

"No, we're not leaving. You can't kill Simmons. We need to see if he's working with anyone or if he's on his own."

Damien turned around to face Kara. "No, that's stupid. We should just kill him and get it over with. Even if he is working with someone, he wouldn't tell us."

"You don't know that. Why does it matter if we try to interrogate him?"

"It's a waste of time."

Kara and Damien continued to argue about the issue for a minute, getting increasingly angry, until…

Raymond pushed Kara and Damien's heads down until they were between their legs and held them there. "He's getting out of his house. Stay down," he warned.

A few moments passed as Raymond held them down in a crouched position and eyed the other side of the street from behind the front seat.

"Can we get up now?"

9

Raymond removed his hands after another few seconds. "Start the car, Damien," he ordered while looking over his shoulder. "He's getting in his car. We have to follow him."

Damien turned the keys in the ignition while he stared at the mirrors and the reflection of Simmons in them. He waited for Simmons to drive by, and then pulled out to follow him.

Kara and Raymond managed to convince Damien to tail Simmons instead of initiating an attack while driving, though it took a few attempts to calm him down.

Damien managed to stay a few cars behind, but still kept up with Simmons. After a few minutes and several turns Damien lost sight of Simmons's car. Kara was able to follow his psychic energy and they caught up again just as Simmons was pulling into an alley.

Damien circled around the alley, and when it was clear that that was where Simmons was heading, they parked the car nearby. They all got out of the car and headed into a small nearby building and up to the roof.

Before they went through the door to access the roof, Damien warned them to be silent. They went out and crept close to the edge of the roof, then got down on their stomachs to peek out over the edge.

Below, they could see Simmons's car parked in the alley. There were no nearby lights, and the buildings around them were either abandoned or closed for the night, as there was no light coming from the windows. The dark of night was nothing to their eyesight, but it still gave a foreboding feeling to the affair. All they could see at their angle was the occasional puff of smoke dancing its way out of the front window of the car, and Simmons's arm flicking the butt to knock the ash off.

"Why is he here, of all places?" Kara whispered.

"Shut up," Damien commanded.

"Maybe it's like you were saying: He's working with someone else," Raymond speculated.

"Shut up," Damien urged louder.

"Maybe they're meeting with him tonight?"

"They could be planning another attack."

Damien placed his hands over Kara's and Raymond's mouths, and then whispered, "There's someone down there."

The Vampire's Victim

Kara's and Raymond's eyes followed Damien's gaze, and they could see a person in the shadows of the alley approaching Simmons's car. Kara shoved Damien's hand off her mouth and focused her attention on the shadowy figure.

There wasn't much to see—the person was wearing an old-fashioned black cloak, but he was tall and muscular. Kara thought it might have been a man, but she couldn't be sure. As the person approached the detective's vehicle, Kara noticed an absence of noise from the figure's footsteps. Even with her superior hearing, she still couldn't register footsteps.

Maybe it's a psychic and they can float? she thought. Kara focussed on the person's feet, and noticed that he was moving his feet like he was walking. *Why would he walk if he was floating already? What kind of a human can move that silently? Unless…* Kara looked over to her companions, and she could tell that they'd come to the same conclusion. The person meeting Simmons might be a vampire. No normal human could be that silent.

Kara, Raymond, and Damien all watched with rapt attention and perked ears as the man entered Simmons's car.

"Saw you this time, you stealthy fuck. Why do you do that all the time, anyway?"

"I do it in case I need to do this," the stranger—it *was* a man—replied.

There was the sound of ripping fabric and then a crunch, all within a few seconds. Simmons coughed and there was a distinct splat of something red against the windshield in front of him. He'd just been stabbed through the stomach, and it had punctured his lungs. Whoever that person was, Simmons knew him, trusted him, and was being killed by him.

"The boss is disappointed in you. We told you not to fail killing the girl this time. Sorry, Simmons. At least you'll make a nice meal."

There was a *thunk* as the unmistakable sound of fangs ramming into flesh met their ears. There was no mistaking it now—the shadow figure was a vampire. A vampire had told Simmons to send psychics after Olivia and the others.

After another moment, the man exited the vehicle and left the alley before Kara, Raymond and Damien could recover from their shock to do anything. When they came out of their stupor, they rose to their feet, collectively jumped down into the alley, and ran over to Simmons's car.

They heard the faint sound of sirens off in the distance, but they couldn't tell if it was headed their way or not. Damien didn't want to take any chances with the police. "We have to get out of here. Being next to a dead detective is not the place to be right now."

Kara slowly walked towards the car and knelt down to look inside. The bloody body of Detective Simmons was sitting in the front seat, his eyes staring straight ahead... until Kara moved into view. Simmons looked over at her.

"Oh my God, he's still alive," she said as her hand instantly covered her mouth.

The other two ignored the possibility of police for the moment and went over next to Kara to see. The detective was barely breathing, sweat covered his forehead, and blood dripped from his mouth and chin. His lips were moving, and it seemed like he was trying to say something.

"Ahh... aaa... faa..." Simmons tried to utter something meaningful, but he didn't have the breath to carry it on. He reached his left hand towards Kara.

The sound of sirens was closer than ever, and the police would be on them in no time.

"We need to leave," Damien insisted.

Kara drew closer to the dying detective. She needed to hear what he was trying to say.

"Kara!" Raymond called.

Kara stepped to the edge of the car, but Simmons didn't have the power. Raymond grabbed Kara's arm, but she wouldn't budge. The detective moved his trembling hand into his jacket pocket and tried to pull something out, but couldn't summon the strength to do so. His hand went limp, and his eyes glassed over.

Kara's jaw dropped. She went inside the car and reached into Simmons's pocket to get what he was holding. It was his phone. She pulled it out and placed it in her pocket.

The others were eyeing her with concern and anger. She started running, and the two followed her. They ran to the other end of the alley where their car was parked. Before they could reach the street, the sound of sirens caught up with them and a police car stopped in front of the vehicle.

Kara looked over her shoulder, and there was another police car on the other end of the alley. Two police officers exited their vehicle at that side,and one of them was talking on their radio.

On their end of the alley, the police exited their car as well, and motioned for Kara, Raymond, and Damien to stop. Both of them had one hand firmly on their guns, but they didn't draw them… yet.

"Stop!" one of them commanded.

Damien tensed, and Kara noticed him clenching his fists. She used her telekinesis to restrain him, and when he noticed he glared at her.

The police came closer, but kept their distance. "Want to tell me why you were running?" one of them asked.

Kara glanced at the others, but her mind was blank. How could they explain what they were doing to get them out of here? *If Olivia was here she'd know just what to say.*

Over the radio on the policeman's shoulder, the other officers said, "Detective Simmons is dead. Take the suspects in for questioning."

One of the police officers pulled out his gun, but kept it aimed at the ground. "Alright, you three, turn around and place your hands up on the wall of that building. You're under arrest," he stated as the second officer pulled out handcuffs.

The police read them their rights, and then Kara, Raymond, and Damien were all arrested and taken away as suspects for a murder they didn't commit.

3. SUSPECTS

"So you're telling me that you just happened upon the detective, and when you heard the sirens your first inclination was to run?"

Kara nodded. "I don't know how many times I have to say it for you to believe me. Check with my friends, they'll back me up. We heard someone scream in the alley so we checked it out, and then we saw the body and heard the sirens. We panicked. I know... it's pathetic," she said with her head downcast.

She was confident that the others would have the same story thanks to low-volume whispers on the ride back to the police station and enhanced hearing. They were able to come up with what to say by the time they reached the station, and the police officers were none the wiser.

The detective interrogating her, Detective Janos, gave her a sceptical and frustrated look. Because there was no blood on them, no weapons, and no eyewitnesses, there was nothing to hold them on.

The detective rose from his seat and excused himself from the room. Kara's hands were shackled to a table in an interrogation room similar to the one she'd rescued Olivia from weeks ago. It was a different station, but they all looked the same to her. Brick and metal framework, wooden doors, and a lingering smell of coffee, ink, gunpowder, and testosterone.

Kara laid her head down on the table to rest, and put her hood up to let the darkness in. It was getting late, and she was growing weary. When she closed her eyes she could see the dead body of Simmons in his car, a red messy hole in his chest, and blood dripping from his chin. It looked like one of her premonitions she usually saw when she foresaw a person's death, but this time it was in the past instead of the future.

The Vampire's Victim

Why couldn't I feel his death approaching? she thought. *Maybe I'm just a shitty psychic and I need to learn how to control my powers better.* Kara rubbed her hair. *Why does it matter anyway? I don't need to save these people. I should be happy that they're dead because less people will come after us.* Kara let out a sigh and laid her cheek on the cold metal table. *But why do I still feel so guilty?*

Olivia's voice came into her head. *"You care too much, Kara."*

"Ye best blacken yer soul," another memory said.

Kara groaned. She knew they were right, but it didn't change how she felt.

The door opening woke Kara up, and she saw the detective who'd been interrogating her enter the room, followed by a uniformed officer. The uniformed officer held keys in his hand, and released her from her bonds.

"You're free to go, but stay in town. We might need you again for further questioning."

Kara nodded as she rubbed her hands where the shackles had been. She walked out of the interrogation room and looked for her friends. She noticed them near an elevator with police escorts. She walked over to them, and they all entered the elevator with two police officers. They rode the elevator in silence, tension palpable in the air.

Upon reaching the bottom floor, officers led them to the exit, then left when they were away from the closed-off areas. The three of them exited the police station, walked a block away, and called for a cab.

"Well, I'm glad that's over with," Raymond commented.

"Just be glad that we weren't charged with anything."

"We wouldn't have even had this issue if you listened to us and ran earlier," Damien shouted.

"I was trying to recover this," she snarled, pulling Simmons's phone out of her pocket.

"Is that…?" Raymond asked while pointing at the phone.

Kara nodded. "This is Simmons's phone, and it's going to help us find out who he was working for, who ordered the hit on Olivia, and maybe who killed him."

Kara pushed the button to turn on the phone, and it immediately went to a lock screen asking for a four-digit passcode. Kara cursed under her breath.

"It's locked," she announced. "Ray, would you be able to get into it?" she asked, offering the phone to him.

Raymond put up his hands. "I'm not that good with tech. I wouldn't know where to start."

Damien scoffed and folded his arms. "Great. We just went through all that trouble, placed targets on our backs for a murder we didn't commit, and for what? We're no further ahead, and it's all your fault." Damien pointed at Kara.

At first, Damien's attack made her want to clutch her heart, but her anger suppressed the ache. "My fault?" she shouted. "It's because of what I did that we even have this, and that we know he was working for someone else." Kara got up in Damien's personal space and jabbed her finger on his chest. "If you had your way you would have killed him on the way to whomever it was he was meeting."

"Then just what do you propose we do now? In your ultimate psychic wisdom, how do we proceed?"

Kara closed her eyes and took a deep breath before opening them again. "As far as I know, there's only one person who can help us unlock the phone and decipher the information inside. I don't like having to ask this person for help, but we have no choice."

...

"So, what brings you to me so late at night?"

Kara, Raymond, and Damien all sat in luxurious seats at a table across from the ever vivacious Vasha. She was wearing a form-fitting purple dress with flowery see-through sleeves, and her hair was up in a loose bun.

Her restaurant was almost empty, and the staff were preparing to close for the night. Her usual bodyguards were standing behind her with their arms folded and a menacing look directed towards the three. One of them flashed his fangs at Raymond, and he cringed.

"We're here because we need help," Kara said.

Vasha raised her brow. "Oh? I'm intrigued. Your group always seems to have the most interesting problems. First a kidnapping, then an assassin. I wonder what new enemy the amazing Kara, vampire-slash-psychic, could have made this time?" she mocked while leaning back in her seat.

16

The Vampire's Victim

"I'm sure you recall our first encounter, when Olivia was taken and held by a psychic detective?" Kara asked.

"Yes, I remember."

Kara pulled out the phone and placed it on the table. "This is the detective's phone. He died... He was killed by someone earlier this night."

Vasha's mouth went flat, and she no longer seemed amused.

"We overheard a conversation before he was killed, and it seemed like the detective was working under someone else."

Vasha crossed her legs and placed her folded hands on her knee. "Were any names mentioned? Did you manage to see the person who killed this detective?"

"No, but we believe the man who killed him was a vampire. He mentioned that the detective would make a good "meal" before he started sucking his blood. That's why we brought you this phone. If we can unlock it there might be a phone number or an email or something that could lead us back to whoever's behind these attacks."

Vasha nodded and picked up the phone. "A plot between psychics and vampires to kill other vampires. Strange indeed," she said as she tapped her sharp nail on the screen of the phone.

For a few seconds, there was only the sound of Vasha's tapping on the screen, until Kara broke the silence.

"Will you help us?"

Vasha stared at Kara for a moment and she almost looked annoyed, but she soon smiled. "Well, I must say, you've piqued my curiosity. I believe I wish to know the answer to this riddle as much as you now." Vasha held up her finger. "But that doesn't mean I will help you without something in return." She pointed at Damien. "You, you are a strapping young vampire with much strength, I can tell. You will owe me a favour, to be used at my discretion. Only then will I help you find this mastermind."

Damien had his brow raised, and he glanced from Vasha to Raymond and Kara. They both nodded to him to go with it. They had discussed the possibility on the drive over, and weighed the pros and cons of owing Vasha another favour. In the face of more attacks and someone dying, owing Vasha seemed light in comparison. Without another word, Damien gave his consent.

After Vasha got Damien's number for his future favour, she rose from her chair with the detective's phone in hand. "I will work on this immediately. You can order something to eat, as this may take some time. Not to worry, it will be on the house," she added with a smile before she turned around and left with her bodyguards. As she moved she told someone to bring them menus and give them whatever they ordered free of charge.

With the mention of food, Kara began noticing how hungry she had gotten. She didn't finish her dinner because Raymond interrupted, and it was past ten at night now. Her stomach grumbled as she actually allowed herself to take in the smells of the gourmet food in the restaurant.

Kara, Raymond, and Damien all ordered something to eat, and servers brought it out to them fresh and hot and to die for. Kara ordered something spicy, her favourite, while Raymond ordered fish and Damien ordered a rare steak.

After they finished eating, their server brought them drinks, but after Kara realised what it was, she declined. Their drinks were wine glasses half-filled with blood. Kara didn't know where the blood was from, and so she didn't drink it. The others gladly drank a free second meal, and complimented the quality of the food.

Kara couldn't help but feel uneasy. Vasha was being almost *too* nice to them, and too cooperative. *It could be just as she said—something like this is unprecedented. If a vampire is helping psychics kill other vampires, Vasha would want to know and stop them... It could also be that she's warming up to me. She was going to cook a meal for Olivia and me that one time.* Kara smiled slightly, and nodded to herself. *Yeah, that must be it.* She shook off the uneasy feeling.

Vasha returned to the dining room and sat back down at the table. Her face was stone, and her expression unreadable. The three waited with bated breath for her to tell them what she'd found, but they all knew better than to rush her.

"Are you sure you want to know? Given what I found, I would suggest backing down."

Kara pursed her lips. "We can't back down, not now."

Vasha nodded. "There were numerous texts back and forth between this Detective Simmons and his handler. The number of the handler belongs to a vampire previously in my employ, but he works for a different vampire now."

Kara's jaw dropped in shock, despite knowing it would be a vampire. "Who does he work for now?"

"Zaal Dalton."

The three were taken aback at the mention of that name. Zaal Dalton was a vampire on the same level as Vasha. He was said to be almost as old as she, and just as powerful, if not more so amongst vampires, because of his work with the Vampire Command.

"But—" Kara began saying.

"Yes," Vasha replied. "Dalton is a staunch pacifist. He's the reason why we aren't warring against psychics right now. It seems that the reason why he's so against us going to war is because he's on the psychics' side." Vasha motioned for one of her bodyguards, and he brought over a folder to her. She took the folder, opened it, and slid it over to them. "I was able to get these emails between several prominent psychics discussing the end of the vampire race—with the exception of Zaal, of course."

Kara took the folder and started flipping through the pages. Raymond and Damien leaned over to look at it as well. The words on the pages painted a clear picture of exactly what Vasha was saying.

Kara looked up from the folder, and Damien took it from her. "But... why? Why would he do this?" Even though she didn't know the man personally, she knew him by reputation, and the reputation was that he wanted the vampire race to survive, and to survive he'd convinced everyone to stop fighting.

Vasha shrugged. "I don't know how you expect me to explain the man's change of heart, but his motives are clearly written on those emails. He wants to survive, and be the only vampire left alive."

Damien threw the folder down on the table, and the papers fell out and scattered across it. "That bastard played everyone for fools while he set up our people to die. Who knows who else he's killed."

Kara wanted to object, but in the face of all the evidence Vasha provided her lips wouldn't move. Her eyes widened as a thought struck her. *That's right, this is Vasha's evidence. What if she's setting Zaal up to take the fall for this so that he's discredited and she can start a new war?* Kara looked straight at Vasha. *Would Vasha do something like that though? I know she's probably hired Dr. Barker-Wilson to research making a weapon against psychics, but it's like Olivia said: it could be for self-defence. What does she gain by creating a new war?*

Vasha noticed Kara's gaze, and she returned it. "In that file I put Zaal's address, should you wish to speak with him, or enact revenge, whatever you desire."

"You're not going to send anyone to stop him?"

Vasha chuckled. "I said before I was intrigued about why a vampire was hiring psychics to kill other vampires. My curiosity is satisfied now, so there's no further meaning to my involvement."

"What if he comes after you?"

Vasha smirked. "I'm perfectly safe; I can assure you of that."

Damien rose from his seat and walked to the exit of the restaurant.

Kara did a double take and called after him before giving Vasha one last look. Vasha still wore the smirk and flashed her fangs as she drank the blood from Kara's wine glass she'd left at the table. Kara couldn't tell if it was a smug smirk of outsmarting someone, or a simple happy smile. She didn't know if she wanted to find out either way.

4. KNEEL BEFORE ZAAL

"All I'm saying is that it's late, and I think we should rest and think things over before we rush in," Kara said.

Kara, Raymond, and Damien were all in Damien's car, driving around aimlessly at this point, trying to decide what to do. Raymond was driving, and Damien and Kara were discussing things in the back seat.

"That's stupid. The longer we wait, the more time Zaal has to prepare another attack. Next you're going to be telling me we shouldn't kill him," Damien shouted.

Kara scratched her face and looked away. "Well…"

Damien's jaw dropped and he scoffed. "This is the person who sent a group of psychics to kill us, who sent an assassin to kill Olivia. Need I remind you that that was the same assassin that nearly killed you as well? What possible reason could you have to let him live?"

Kara summoned her courage and stared straight at Damien. "Because we don't know if what Vasha said was the truth. Something about how she was acting seemed… off."

Damien gave Kara a doubtful look, and then his phone tinged, indicating a text message. He took it out and looked at it. He seemed to be checking out of the conversation.

After a moment, Kara spoke up. "Well, what are you thinking?"

Damien stared at the screen of the phone for another moment. "What do you suggest we do when we meet with Zaal?"

"Let's just talk with him, get his side of the story, and then go from there. Maybe we can bring what Vasha gave us to the Command and have them investigate it."

Damien put away his phone, looked at Kara, then turned away and stared out the window. "Fine, we'll sleep on it, and then in the morning we can follow your lead."

Kara let out a breath she had been holding. "Thank you, Damien," she said while touching his arm.

Damien looked at her hand, then at her, and then went back to glancing at the passing cars. He appeared deep in thought, with his muscular arm resting on the doorframe and his hand under his chin.

The group were silent for the remainder of the car ride, as they headed back to where Raymond had parked near Simmons's apartment. After giving Damien back his keys, Raymond and Kara went to his vehicle and he drove Kara home.

She checked her phone, and noticed that it was almost midnight now. She entered her apartment trying not to make any noise so that Mr. Montgomery wouldn't wake up. She thought it might be a futile effort though. Mr. Montgomery seemed to always hear her when she arrived late.

Sure enough, just as she was closing the door, she could hear him shuffling in his favourite chair. She saw him waking up and donning his glasses, and noticed the television was still playing. *He must have stayed up waiting for me.*

"That you, Kara?" he asked.

"Yes, it's me Mr. Montgomery," she replied.

She noticed that the dishes she'd left on the table were cleared, and the crock-pot full of chili was off the counter, presumably in the fridge. Mr. Montgomery even managed to clean up after her.

Kara smiled. "Come on, let's get you to bed." She went over to Magnus and helped him out of the chair.

"I don't need your help," he stated, but he didn't pull away.

Kara kept her hand entwined in his, despite his assertion. "I know."

She guided Magnus to his room, and helped him into bed before saying goodnight to him and heading to her room.

Kara lay down on her bed and tried to decode the conversations she'd had over the day. From Simmons's failed dying words, to Vasha's expressions, and Damien's shutting down on the car ride. She didn't know whom to trust, but she did know that she wanted to talk with Zaal and see what he had to say.

After some time thinking it over, Kara sat up in her bed. *I only have one chance to ask him the questions I want.*

She got out of bed and sneaked out of the apartment, the file folder Vasha had given her in hand. Once on street level, she opened the folder and took note of the address before calling a cab to drive her there. After a few minutes, the cab came and drove her to Zaal Dalton's address.

After a twenty-minute drive into a secluded neighbourhood, the cab dropped Kara off in front of what she could only describe as a castle.

Dalton's mansion was made of brick and even from Kara's vantage point at the far end of a long driveway she could tell it was massive. The grounds were like something out of a movie, with fresh-cut grass, evergreen trees and bushes, and a fountain just in front of the door. The mansion itself had several floors and windows covered by thick blinds.

He won't have to worry about burns in the summer with blinds like those.

Kara paid the cabbie and exited the vehicle. She took one last longing look at the mansion before the cab sped off. She went up to the gate and pressed on the intercom button to see if anyone would answer.

As she waited for the intercom to ring back, Kara looked around the large front gate—it looked ajar, but she couldn't be sure. She went over and pulled on the iron bars, and it swung open. The lock keeping it in place was broken.

She immediately looked over to the mansion, and then at the silent intercom. Something felt amiss.

Kara opened the gate and entered the driveway. As soon as she entered, she noticed something poking out of a nearby bush. She went closer to see what it was, and noticed the dead bodies of two guards.

She gasped at the sight, and her thoughts went to how Damien was acting on the car ride. He received a text, and then stopped arguing with her. *Did he agree with me so that he could come here on his own and kill Dalton?* She gritted her teeth. *Damn it, Damien!*

Kara focussed her mind and encompassed her body with the barrier of power. After she formed her shield, she ran with all her speed to the mansion's entrance. She ran up the side of the fountain and jumped over the water in a straight line towards the door.

The doors were wide open, the hinges busted off, and she could see the inside. She slowed down and cautiously entered the main hall.

The main hall of the mansion was empty and expansive. Beneath Kara's feet there was a mosaic painted on the floor, and to the front a large extravagant staircase leading up to the second floor. Dozens of paintings and other ornaments covered the walls and spoke to the riches the owner held.

Kara noticed blood on the floor near the stairs, then another splatter on the railing. She followed the blood to the second floor and into a hallway. The mansion was eerily quiet and empty. Her own footsteps echoed off the walls and made it sound like someone was walking behind her. Every inch forward had her looking over her shoulder and jumping at shadows.

She walked through the hallway, passing by a multitude of doors and marble statues and mounted weapons.

The smell of blood drew her along, and at the end of the hallway she went to the right and up another set of stairs. The trail led her to the top, down another hall, and to a room.

She held the doorknob and took in a deep breath to concentrate her mind. She was ready to send a blast of psychic energy at whatever she saw beyond the door. She turned the knob and pushed the door open.

In the room—a study, judging by the large bookcases and chairs and fireplace—she saw Damien lying in one of the chairs. He was bleeding from his mouth and chest, and his eyes were closed.

Kara screamed his name, rushed over, and knelt down next to him. When she placed her hands over his, he woke with a start and flung his hand towards her neck. Her psychic barrier protected her from his strike.

"Damien, it's me," she coaxed.

The Vampire's Victim

Damien's eyes, though tired, lost their glaze as he focussed on her face. When he realised who it was, his hand flopped down on the arm of the chair.

"Kara, what…?" Damien coughed up more blood. "What are you doing here?"

"I came to talk with Dalton, and then I saw the gate was broken and the guards were killed." She gripped Damien's hands and shook them as she closed her eyes. "Why couldn't you just wait? Why…?"

Damien didn't respond for a moment. "Because I knew you didn't have the power to do what's necessary. I didn't want you put into a position that you couldn't handle."

"What position? The position of killing someone for no good God-damn reason?"

Damien managed to muster some strength back into his words. "How about trying to kill my friends. Isn't that good enough reason?"

"We don't… you don't know that he's the one behind this."

Damien gave a weak laugh. "That was always the thing that annoyed me about you: you're too naive." Despite his words, Damien's voice was soft and sounded like the old Damien, before he'd known she was a psychic.

When Kara looked up at Damien to respond, his eyes widened, but he wasn't looking at her. He was looking behind her. Kara turned her head to look over her shoulder. Damien wrapped his arms around her and pulled her back. Together, the two of them fell back in the chair. Kara felt a pressure of wind along the back of her head and neck as if something flashed by her.

Dalton's attacking us!

Instinct kicked in and when Damien and she hit the floor she rolled over to the side and thrust her hand out. She sent a psychic wave at the attacker with more force than she had ever mustered before. The blast made contact, and Kara was only able to register Zaal Dalton's eyes widening as the psychic energy forced him back. Dalton flew towards the other end of the mansion. Kara gritted her teeth and continued pushing with all her might. She wasn't able to see Dalton, but she could hear the sound of him crashing into wall after wall of stone towards the end of the mansion. She relaxed her mind and lowered the psychic wave after a moment.

Kara jumped to her feet and helped Damien up from the overturned chair. "C'mon, we need to get moving. If he's any bit the vampire everyone says he was, that didn't kill him."

When Damien tried to stand on his feet, he doubled over and coughed. A spurt of blood burst from his mouth. Kara used her powers to seal the wounds on the outside of Damien, and to support his legs so he could stand.

"Were you trying to kill him?" he asked.

Kara put his arm over her shoulder. "No."

She pulled Damien along, and they exited the other side of the study and into the hall again.

"This way," Damien said as he pointed to the right and down the hall.

Kara looked over to where he was pointing, and it was a dead end. "But that way is the entrance," she said, pointing to where she'd come from.

"Trust me," he replied.

Kara looked over at Damien, and in his eyes she saw some sort of determination. It was the same determination that she'd admired about him and fallen in love with so long ago.

She guided Damien over to the end of the hallway. Damien lifted his free hand and started to touch the wall. He tilted his head, and Kara could see he was sniffing the air. She looked at the wall and mimicked him.

Blood! And not Damien's. But where is it coming from?

As if to answer her, Damien punched the wall in front of them. The bricks of the mansion fell apart and revealed an opening with a spiral staircase leading down.

After the bricks fell open, the smell of blood grew stronger. Kara used her telekinesis to break through the rest of the bricks, and the two of them entered the secret room.

Before heading down the stairs, Kara turned around and fixed the wall from the inside as best she could. *It won't fool the master of the house, but it might buy us some time.*

The Vampire's Victim

Kara and Damien headed down the rusted iron spiral staircase as quickly as they could, given Damien's wounds. The smells of the old brick, flaking rust, and intoxicating blood mixed together and gave the area an ancient feel. The castle was older than it looked, but the inside of this room revealed its true colors.

At the bottom of the staircase there was a wooden door with a brass handle. Kara touched the brass and her senses kicked in. From the room beyond she could sense a lingering feeling of longing and pride. It was the faintest of emotions, nothing like the guilt she'd felt from the Celtic Butcher's home, but it was still there.

Kara ignored the memory and opened the door. Damien and Kara entered the room, and the scent of blood hit them in a wave.

The room was a long wine cellar of brick and stone. The cellar had to be sealed, considering the stale smell of the air and the lingering blood, but as with most cellars the stone floor was perpetually damp. The source of the coppery smell came from the wine racks which, instead of wine, held bottles of blood on their arched frames. In one corner of the cellar there was a fireplace with an ornate chair and an end table in front of it. On the end table there was a wine glass and a book gathering dust. The longing and pride Kara felt was emanating from those items.

Damien brought Kara back to the here and now when he reached out and grabbed a bottle of blood and started drinking from it.

"What are you doing?" she asked in a harsh whisper.

"I'm trying to recover."

"We should be getting out of here, not drinking."

"You still think we have a chance to leave? No matter where we go now, Dalton is going to come after us. We need to kill him."

"No, we don't," Kara replied. She grabbed the bottle from Damien and put it back on the shelf. The blood called to her, but she ignored it.

Kara pulled Damien back and started dragging him through the cellar. *There must be another way out.*

She and Damien went between a set of wine racks towards the back of the room. The low ceiling and poor lighting at the back didn't give much visibility, even for their eyes. When they reached the end of the rack, they looked to their left and right, but there was no exit, only brick walls.

"You won't find escape there," a voice said from behind them.

Damn! Kara turned around, and Zaal Dalton was at the entrance of the wine cellar.

Zaal Dalton, the infamous ancient vampire, had a face like pure snow, and his jet-black hair was slicked back in stark contrast. His eyes, though menacing, looked as though he was just as confused by Kara and Damien being there as he was angry. He was favouring his left leg, and there was a cut in his side with a smudge of blood on his white dress shirt.

Kara put a barrier up in front of her and Damien. "Please stop, my friend made a mistake. He thought that you were involved in an attack against our companions. If you just let us leave, then we'll forget this happened."

Dalton gritted his teeth. "Hmph. A likely ploy. Once I put my guard down, then you attack again. I saw your friend's phone. Vasha sent you to kill me. There's no use denying it." Dalton pulled out a phone from his pocket, the same model as Damien's. "I don't know why a psychic is working for her, but after I dispose of you I will find out what she's planning this time."

Kara's jaw dropped and she glanced from the phone to Damien. His pursed lips and stone-straight stare said everything. *Could it have been Vasha's favour? That's why he was so docile on the car ride. He received a text from Vasha right beforehand.*

Kara turned around, and Dalton was ten feet from them, right in front of her barrier. Their eyes met, and his brows furrowed. Her mind went numb from his gaze. He was using the same power as Vasha on her. Her barrier broke as she went into a slight daze.

Before she could recover, Dalton sprung forward and slashed at her. Damien moved his arm away from her shoulder and pushed her off to the side. Dalton's hand came down and sliced at Damien's elbow. The razor-sharp claws ripped through his skin, and blood took its place. Damien fell to the floor and clutched his arm while suppressing a scream of pain.

The Vampire's Victim

Dalton stepped forward and raised his hand again, aiming to strike Damien one final time.

"Stop!" Kara screamed. She tackled Dalton and the two tumbled across the damp stone of the cellar.

Kara scrambled to her knees and held up her hand. She sent a probe into the depths of her mind, but the fog was still there. She could feel that it wasn't as thick or as penetrating as Vasha's power, but she still wasn't able to summon her powers. "Please stop," she begged. "We aren't with Vasha, we—"

Dalton's hand gripped her throat and snuffed out her voice. "Enough of your lies," he seethed.

She tried to force words out through her constricted neck, trying to tell Dalton about the allegations, but they wouldn't come. *Would he even listen if I could tell him?*

She pulled on his fingers, holding his full strength at bay and keeping herself alive. His gaze still suppressed her powers. She couldn't hold him back forever with her level of strength, and the lack of oxygen was getting to her. Her throat hurt, her eyes watered, and she was feeling fatigued.

"Pl... please..." she croaked.

Dalton didn't respond, and the cold look on his face didn't change with her plea. The confusion she saw earlier was gone, replaced by anger and excitement. Kara felt like she was witnessing something few people saw before they died: an ancient vampire's bloodlust.

The edges of Kara's vision began to fade. Black pulsed in on all sides with every slow beat of her heart. She could feel her heart throbbing in her ears as it lost its tempo. She was losing consciousness, and losing her life.

Dalton pulled one of his hands back, and still maintained his hold on Kara's neck. He was about to send his razor-sharp claws through her stomach, impaling her. Without her powers to protect her, she would be killed.

Dalton went for the killing blow.

Damien punched Dalton in the back of the knee. Dalton's balance crumbled and he went to one knee. His nails slashed the side of Kara's stomach a quarter inch in. Blood surged from Kara's stomach, and the pain was immediate and overwhelming even at the edge of unconsciousness. If her throat would have allowed it, she would have screamed.

Dalton's grip on Kara's neck never weakened despite Damien's attack, and he looked over his shoulder before kicking Damien in the face. When Dalton looked away, though, the power of his gaze faltered, and she felt her psychic energy returning. She used that time to enhance her strength, protect her neck and body, and close the wound on her stomach. She coughed as she tried to pull air into a damaged wind-pipe. Her vision and consciousness returned in a flash.

Dalton turned back around and stared at Kara with his psychic-suppressing eyes again. She felt a haze creeping its way back into her mind, and her psychic powers dulling, but she pushed back against it. She forced her eyes open wide and returned Dalton's stare back at him. It took all her concentration just to keep from losing the protection on her neck, but she knew from experience it was possible to break whatever power he and Vasha used.

Kara focussed on Dalton and pushed against him with her telekinesis. The memory of near death, the pain on her stomach, and adrenaline drove her mind to fight, and all thoughts of flight were gone.

There was something else that drove Kara to fight, and she didn't understand it. She felt a passionate rage bubbling within her unlike anything she had felt before. With the return of her powers, staring into Dalton's eyes, into the eyes of death, she felt like she wanted to fight.

She wanted to kill, and the feeling was overwhelming her.

Kara and Dalton fought a stationary battle. She pushed against him with her psychic powers, and he focussed his penetrating gaze on her to suppress her. To an onlooker it would seem like they were only staring at each other, but the exchange of force was plain to feel in the air around them.

Sweat beads formed on their foreheads and snaked down the sides of their cheeks and noses before falling to the stone floor of the cellar. Their teeth were clenched, their brows furrowed, and their muscles taut as each strained themselves for supremacy.

With each passing second, the feelings inside Kara intensified and enhanced her psychic prowess. She couldn't even feel the wound on her stomach anymore. When she'd faced the Celtic Butcher, she'd still been fatigued from stopping his bullet, but now she was fresh and focussed. She was stronger than his gaze, she could feel it.

Kara broke Dalton's hands free from her neck. His hands were thrust to his sides from her enhanced strength. She used her telekinesis to lift him in the air and made a similar choking gesture as he did. Dalton gripped at his neck, trying to pull against the invisible force pressing on his wind-pipe. The anger in his eyes faded and fear took its place when his struggles bore no fruit.

Kara squeezed tighter and tighter with her powers. She could feel his muscles contracting under the weight she applied, the bones bending under her control. She was stronger than his vampire body, she could feel it.

A piercing crack echoed in the cellar. Dalton's head went limp and his chin hit his chest. His neck had snapped under the stress of Kara's psychic binding. The glazed look that passed over his eyes told her he was dead, even if his posture hadn't already.

She'd killed Zaal Dalton, just as Vasha had wanted her to.

Kara dropped the arched body of her victim to the floor and he hit it with a thud. His arms and legs fell into odd angles; he looked like a ragdoll.

She caught her breath, and the adrenaline subsided. The battle was over, and her body no longer needed it. Despite the adrenaline leaving and her previous excitement and anger waning, Kara didn't feel anything from committing murder.

It was not more than a week ago that she'd openly wept over the death of someone she hardly knew. Now, she'd killed someone and she didn't feel anything close to the guilt she knew she should have.

Kara looked at her trembling hands. They were shaking, but not out of fear or remorse. *Why?* she thought. *Why don't I feel the same? What's wrong with me?*

Her gaze moved to Damien, who was still lying unconscious on the floor of the cellar. She shook her head and pushed away the confusion, and then picked him up off the stone.

She used her powers to hold his wounds closed as best she could, and also to carry him over to the exit of the blood cellar. Before she went though the cellar door, she took one last look at the vampire she'd killed.

As she climbed the rusty spiral staircase and left the castle-like mansion with Damien in tow, another question lingered in her mind: Had Dalton really been behind everything, or did Vasha lie to them so they would kill him?

Kara decided then and there that she would find the answer, no matter the cost.

THE END

ABOUT THE AUTHOR

Shawn Wiseman credits his love of reading and writing to his parents, who taught him how to read from an early age, and fostered his creativity.

After almost becoming a boring businessman, Shawn decided to try his hand at writing, and found his passion. He likes strong characters, lots of action, and punchy dialogue. Some of his vices include video games, swearing like a sailor, and fast food.

Shawn gets inspiration from his friends and family who continue to encourage him with his writing. Before trying his hand at self-publishing, a friend was the one who convinced him to try a writing challenge, and he hasn't looked back since then. His biggest goal is to create characters and stories that will inspire others to try their hand at writing, just as he was inspired before.

It would help Shawn out if you shared this novel with your friends or leave a review on Amazon.